W9-CRM-504

ZOMBIES REST IN PEACE

by Leah Kaminski

illustrated by Jared Sams

Torch Graphic Press

Published in the United States of America by Cherry Lake Publishing Group
Ann Arbor, Michigan
www.cherrylakepublishing.com

Reading Adviser: Marla Conn, MS, Ed., Literacy specialist, Read-Ability, Inc.

Book Design: Book Buddy Media

Photo Credits: page 1: ©vi73777/iStock / Getty Images; page 7: ©omyos/iStock / Getty Images; page 9: ©CSA Images/Vetta / Getty Images; page 15: ©JonkersElias / Pixabay; page 27: ©blamb/ iStock / Getty Images; page 30: ©Jadvani_Shared / Pixabay; background: ©MR.Cole_Photographer/ Moment / Getty Images; background: ©Dima Viunnyk/Moment / Getty Images (sidebars); background: ©OpenClipart-Vectors / Pixabay (facts); background: ©MarjanNo / Pixabay (lined paper)

Torch Graphic Press is an imprint of Cherry Lake Publishing Group.

Library of Congress Cataloging-in-Publication Data
Names: Kaminski, Leah, author. | Sams, Jared, illustrator.
Title: Zombies rest in peace / by Leah Kaminski ; illustrated by Jared Sams.
Description: Ann Arbor, Michigan : Torch Graphic Press, 2020. | Series: The Secret Society
    of Monster Hunters | Includes bibliographical references and index. | Audience: Ages 10-
    13. | Audience: Grades 4-6. | Summary: Jorge, Marcus, and Elena travel to Ottumwa, Iowa,
    in 1983, to locate a flock of zombies at one of the first video game competitions.
Identifiers: LCCN 2020016507 (print) | LCCN 2020016508 (ebook) | ISBN 9781534169449 (hardcover) |
    ISBN 9781534171121 (paperback) | ISBN 9781534172968 (pdf) | ISBN 9781534174801 (ebook)
Subjects: LCSH: Graphic novels. | CYAC: Graphic novels. |
    Zombies—Fiction. | Time travel—Fiction. | Secret societies—Fiction.
Classification: LCC PZ7.7.K355 Zo 2020 (print) | LCC PZ7.7.K355 (ebook) | DDC 741.5/973—dc23
LC record available at https://lccn.loc.gov/2020016507
LC ebook record available at https://lccn.loc.gov/2020016508

Cherry Lake Publishing Group would like to acknowledge the work of the Partnership for 21st Century Learning, a Network of Battelle for Kids. Please visit http://www.battelleforkids.org/networks/p21 for more information.

Printed in the United States of America
Corporate Graphics

TABLE OF CONTENTS

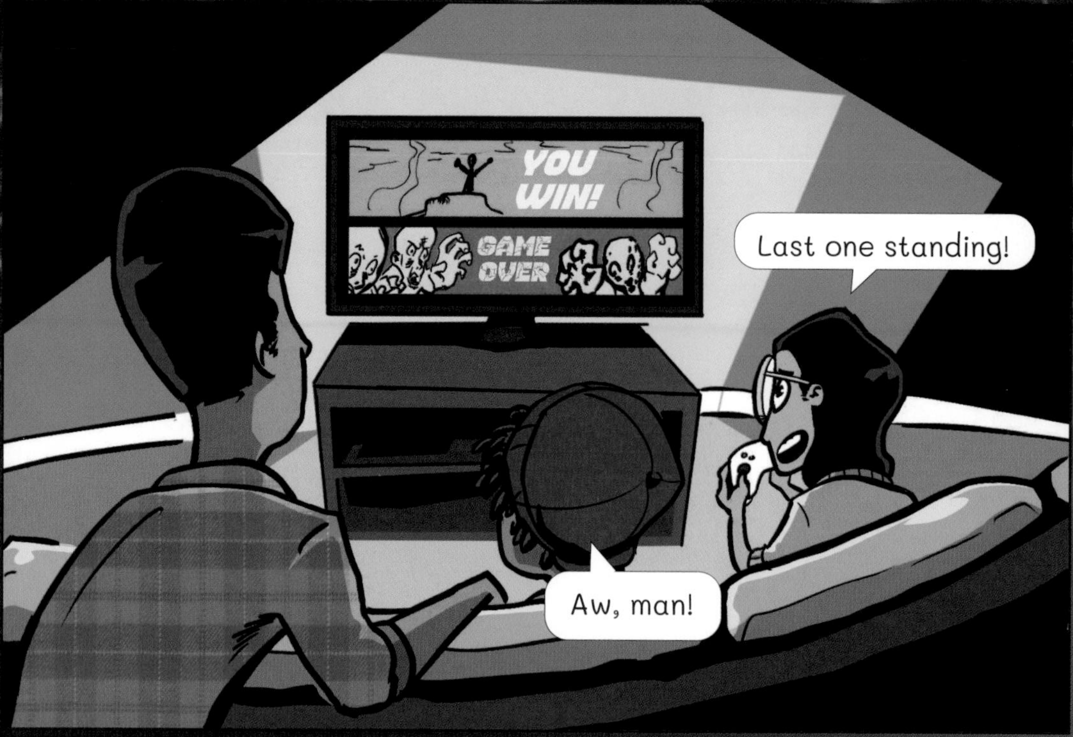

YOU WIN!
GAME OVER
Last one standing!
Aw, man!

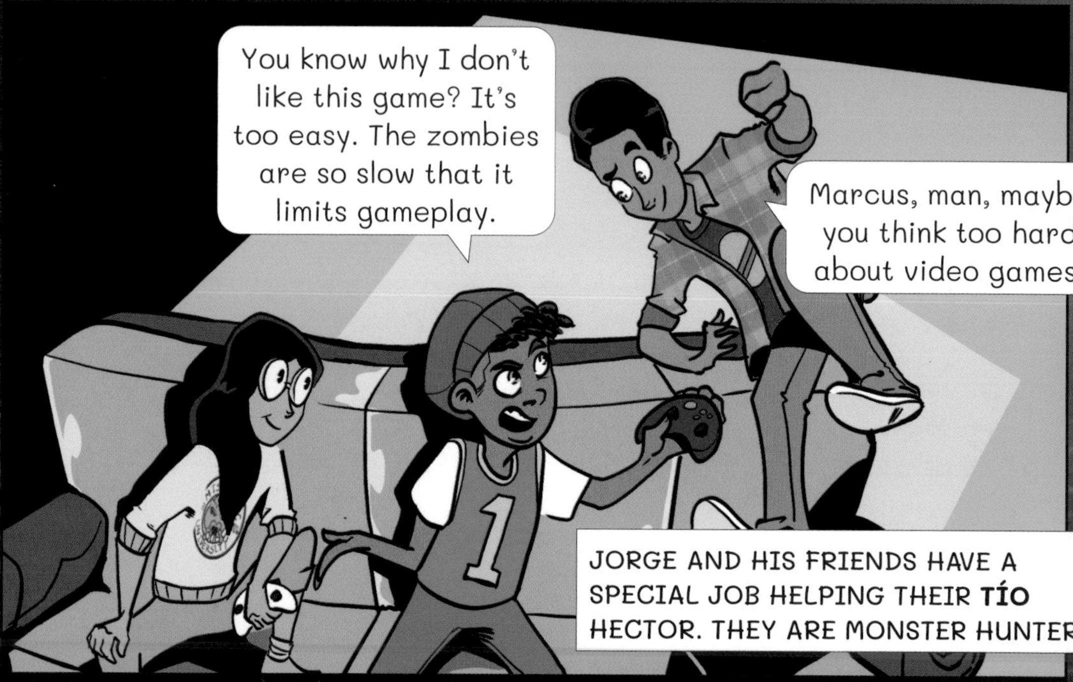

You know why I don't like this game? It's too easy. The zombies are so slow that it limits gameplay.
Marcus, man, maybe you think too hard about video games.
JORGE AND HIS FRIENDS HAVE A SPECIAL JOB HELPING THEIR **TÍO** HECTOR. THEY ARE MONSTER HUNTERS.

tío: Spanish for "uncle"

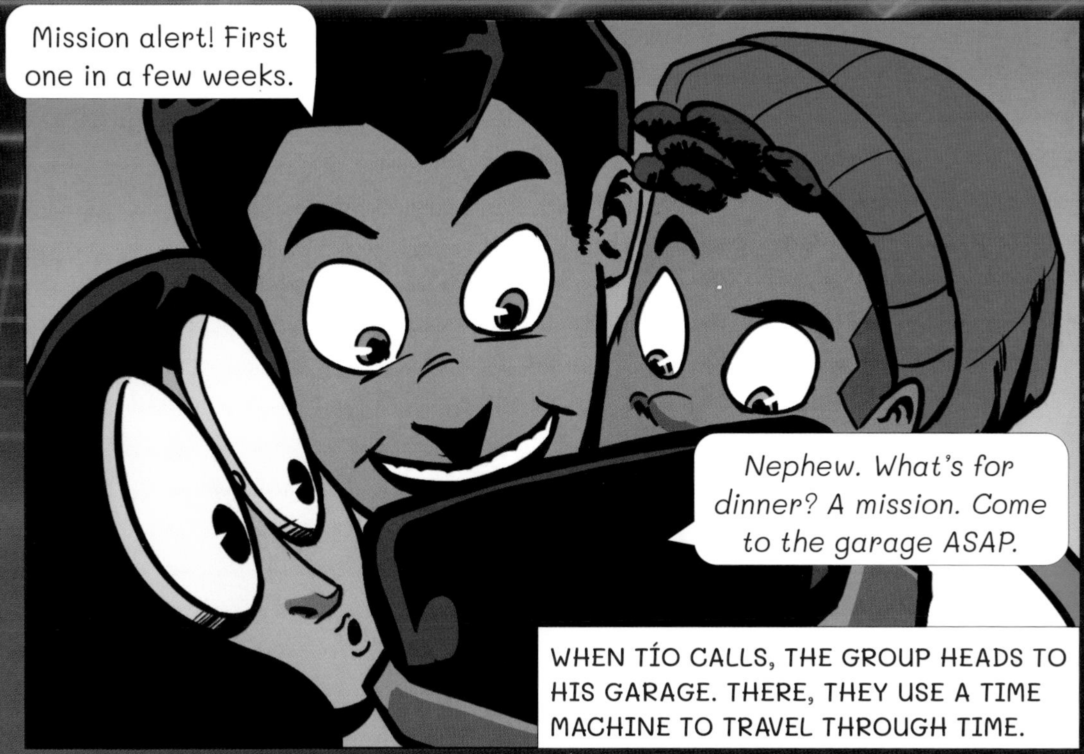
Mission alert! First one in a few weeks.
Nephew. What's for dinner? A mission. Come to the garage ASAP.
WHEN TÍO CALLS, THE GROUP HEADS TO HIS GARAGE. THERE, THEY USE A TIME MACHINE TO TRAVEL THROUGH TIME.

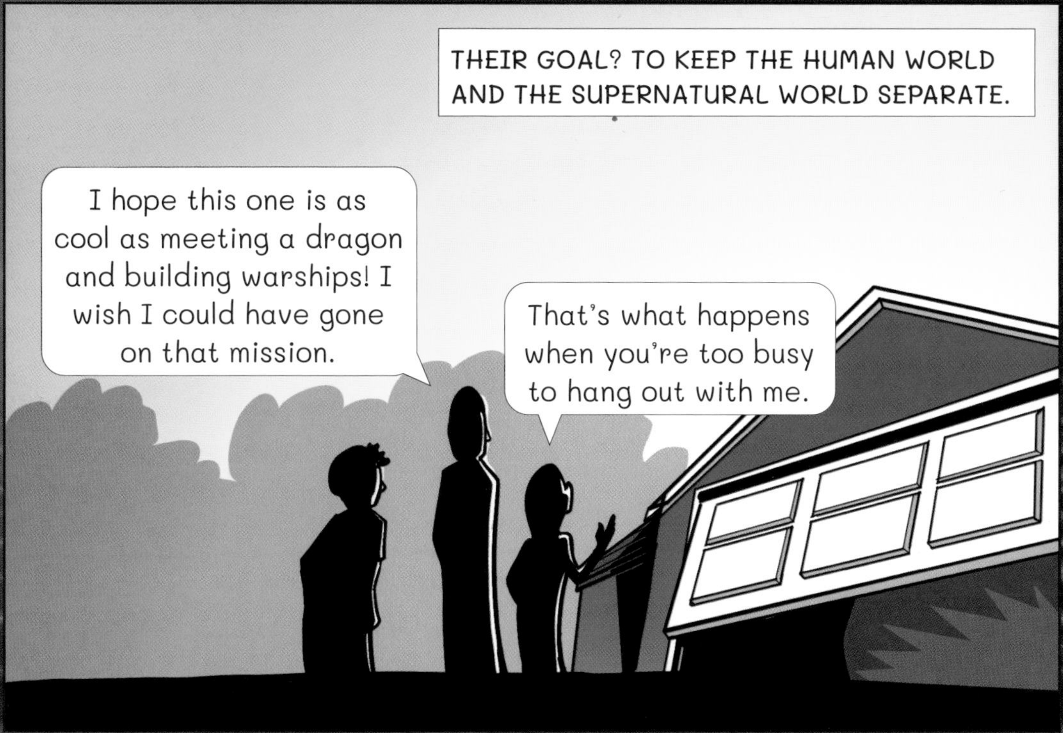
THEIR GOAL? TO KEEP THE HUMAN WORLD AND THE SUPERNATURAL WORLD SEPARATE.
I hope this one is as cool as meeting a dragon and building warships! I wish I could have gone on that mission.
That's what happens when you're too busy to hang out with me.

I'm sending you to Ottumwa, Iowa, 1983.

We're going to... *Iowa*?

In the fantastic year of... *1983*?

Hey now. What if I told you it was called "the Video Game Capital of the World" back then?

Cool!

What are we waiting for?

This mission is dangerous, though, and you need to be calm and have your **wits** about you. Because... you're hunting a zombie.

Zombies are unintelligent, and very dangerous...

wits: mental sharpness

TIPS FOR THE DECADE

The 1980s were a time of great change in the United States. The Cold War was still a problem, but the economy grew under presidents Ronald Reagan and George H.W. Bush. **Income inequality** was beginning to increase. And people became more concerned with things that they wanted to buy. It is sometimes called "the Greed Decade" for these reasons.

* Computer technology was advancing.
* Personal computers (PCs) were invented.
* For the first time, many people could watch movies on **VCRs** and play video games on their PCs.

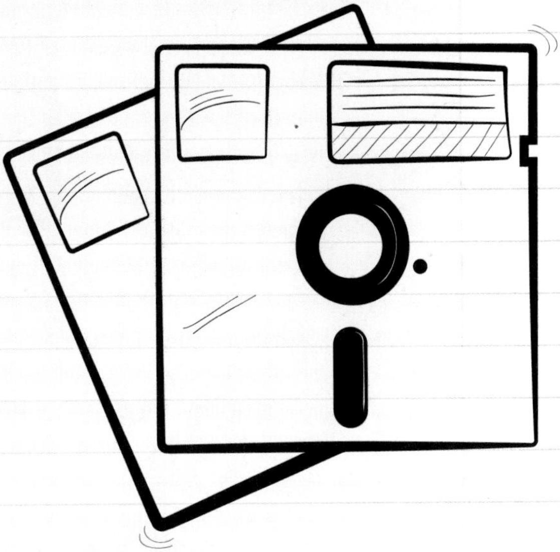

income inequality: the gap between the richest people and the poorest people

VCRs: videocassette recorders used for recording shows off of a television or [redacted]

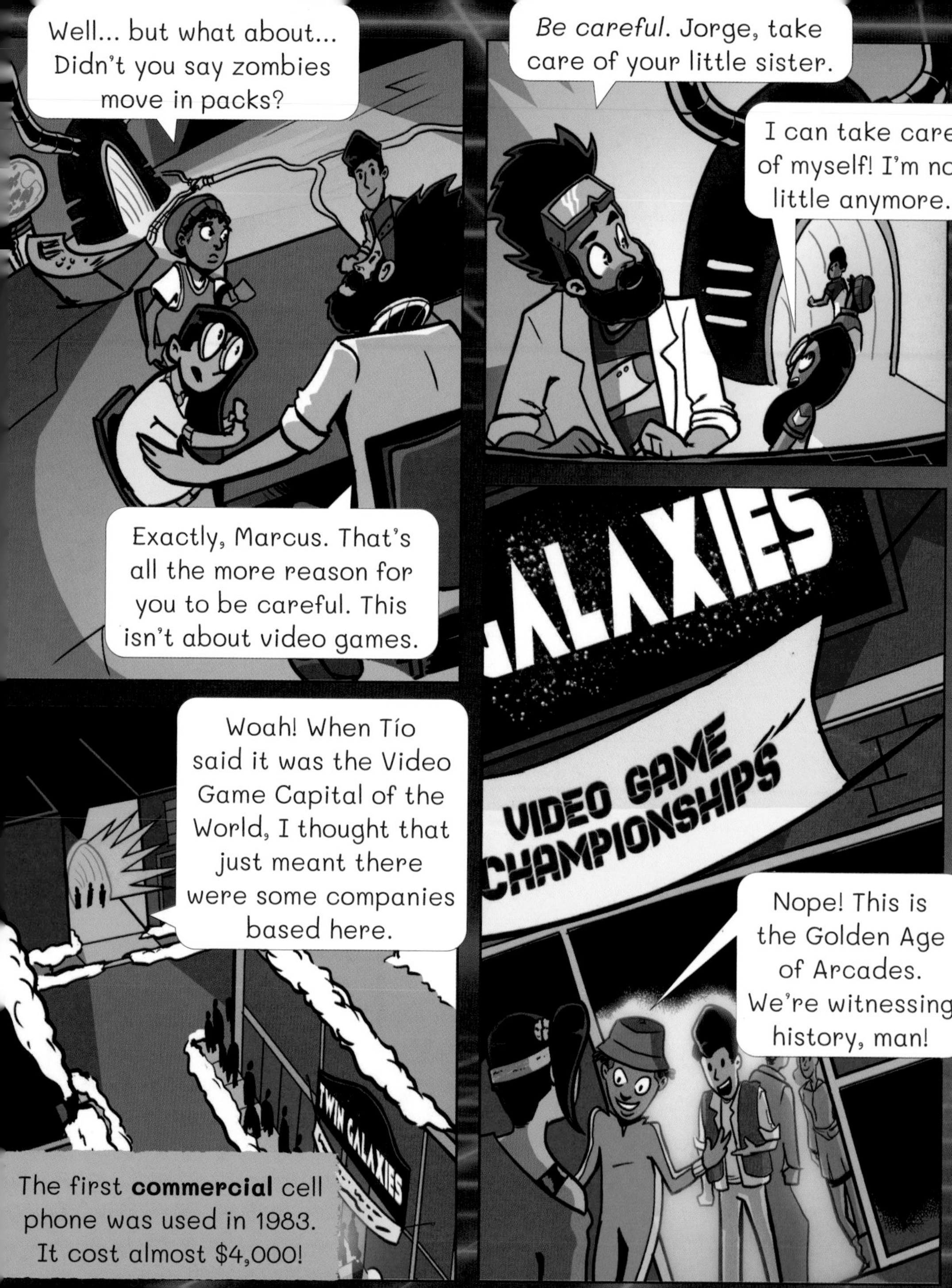

Well... but what about... Didn't you say zombies move in packs?
Exactly, Marcus. That's all the more reason for you to be careful. This isn't about video games.
Be careful. Jorge, take care of your little sister.
I can take care of myself! I'm not little anymore.
Woah! When Tío said it was the Video Game Capital of the World, I thought that just meant there were some companies based here.
TWIN GALAXIES
The first **commercial** cell phone was used in 1983. It cost almost $4,000!
GALAXIES
VIDEO GAME CHAMPIONSHIPS
Nope! This is the Golden Age of Arcades. We're witnessing history, man!

PACKING LIST

By the end of the 1980s, fashion was big, bright, and bold. Big hair, big shoulder pads, bright makeup, and lots of accessories were in style. In the early 80s, athletic wear was in fashion. Sneakers, striped athletic socks, headbands, and leg warmers were popular with both men and women. Acid wash jeans and all-denim outfits were also in.

Turtlenecks and trench coats were worn in cooler weather, as were puffer jackets and puffer vests. "Glam rock" outfits worn by singers like Cyndi Lauper and Joan Jett were popular with some teens too.

* Converse high-top sneakers
* Acid-wash jeans
* Puffer coat
* Leg warmers
* Rubik's Cube
* A copy of *Teen Beat* magazine
* Walkman—with cassette tapes!

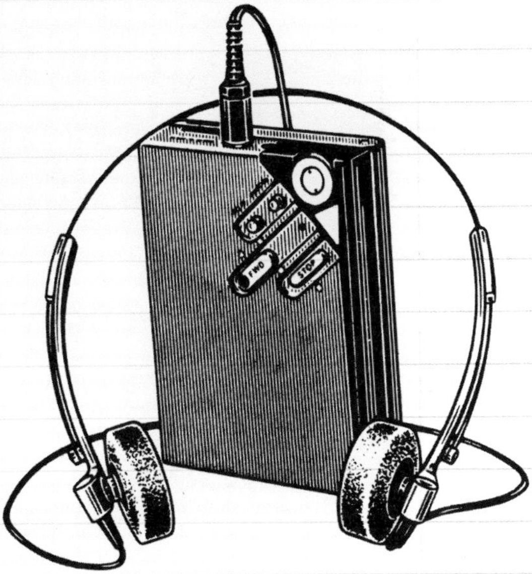
FWD
STOP

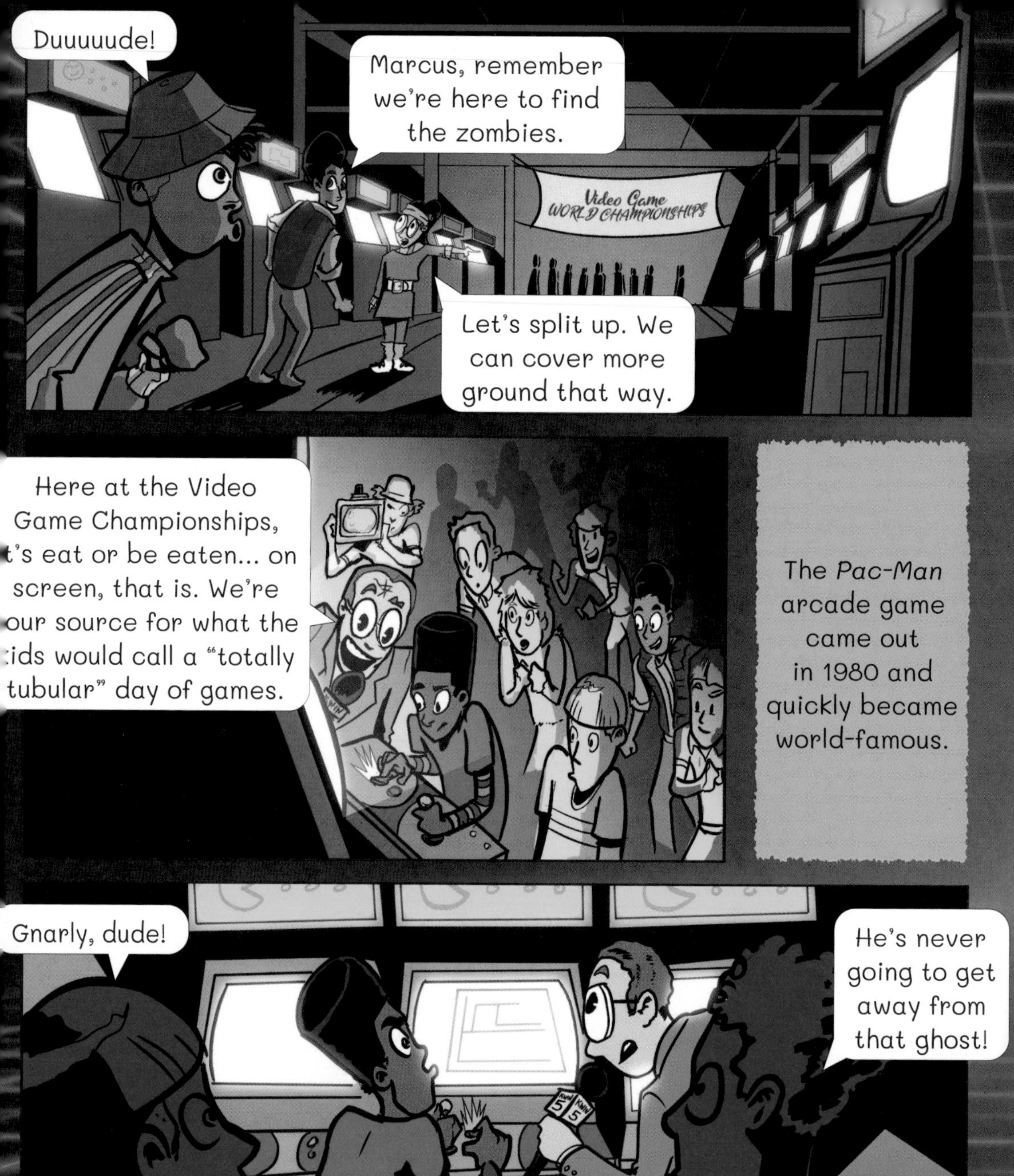
Duuuuude!
Marcus, remember we're here to find the zombies.
Video Game WORLD CHAMPIONSHIPS
Let's split up. We can cover more ground that way.
Here at the Video Game Championships, t's eat or be eaten... on screen, that is. We're our source for what the ids would call a "totally tubular" day of games.
The *Pac-Man* arcade game came out in 1980 and quickly became world-famous.
Gnarly, dude!
He's never going to get away from that ghost!

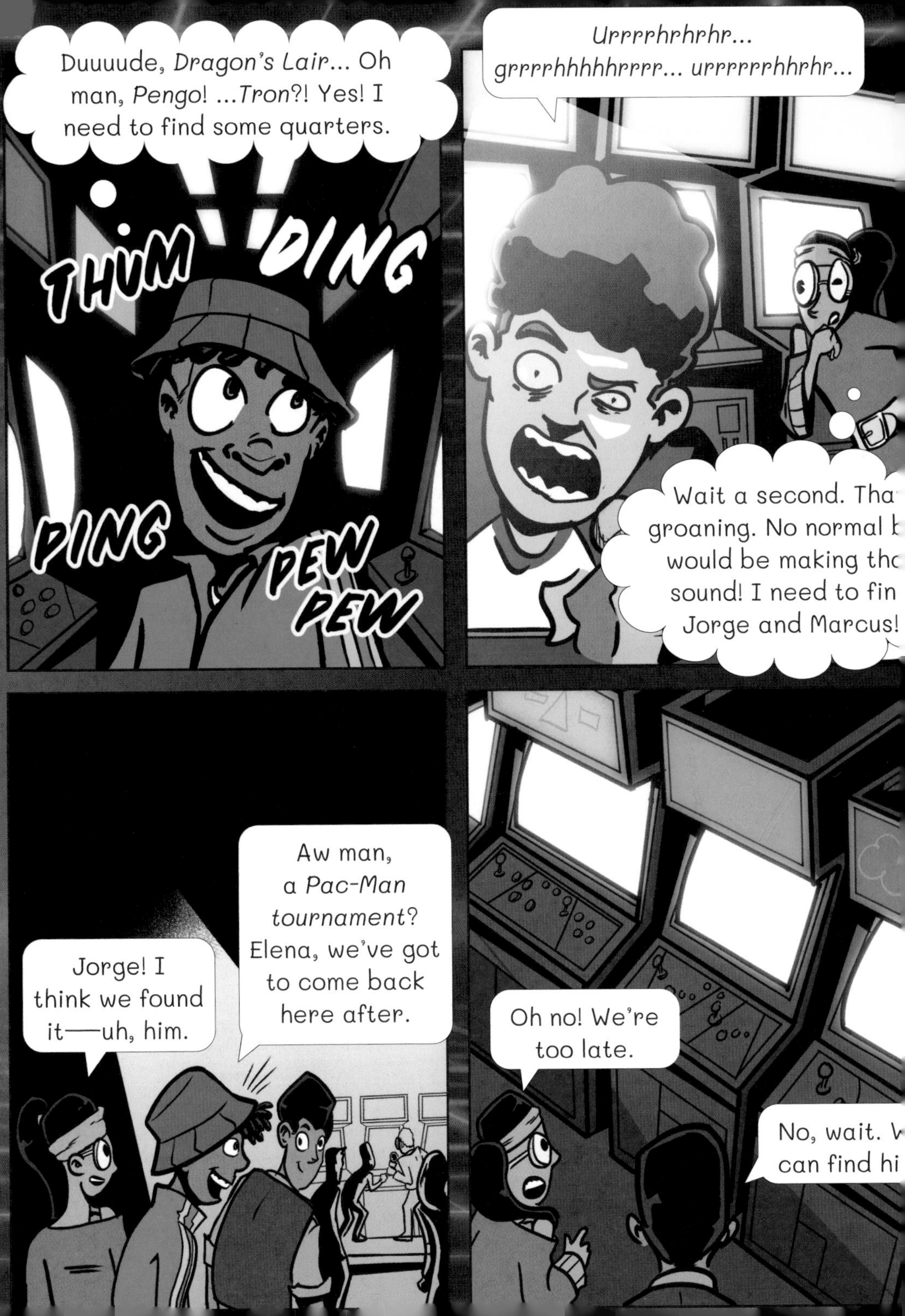
Duuuude, *Dragon's Lair*... Oh man, *Pengo*! ...*Tron*?! Yes! I need to find some quarters.
THUM
DING
DING
PEW PEW
Urrrrhrhrhr... grrrrhhhhhrrrr... urrrrrrhhrhr...
Wait a second. Tha
groaning. No normal
would be making th
sound! I need to fin
Jorge and Marcus!
Jorge! I think we found it—uh, him.
Aw man, a *Pac-Man tournament*? Elena, we've got to come back here after.
Oh no! We're too late.
No, wait.
can find hi

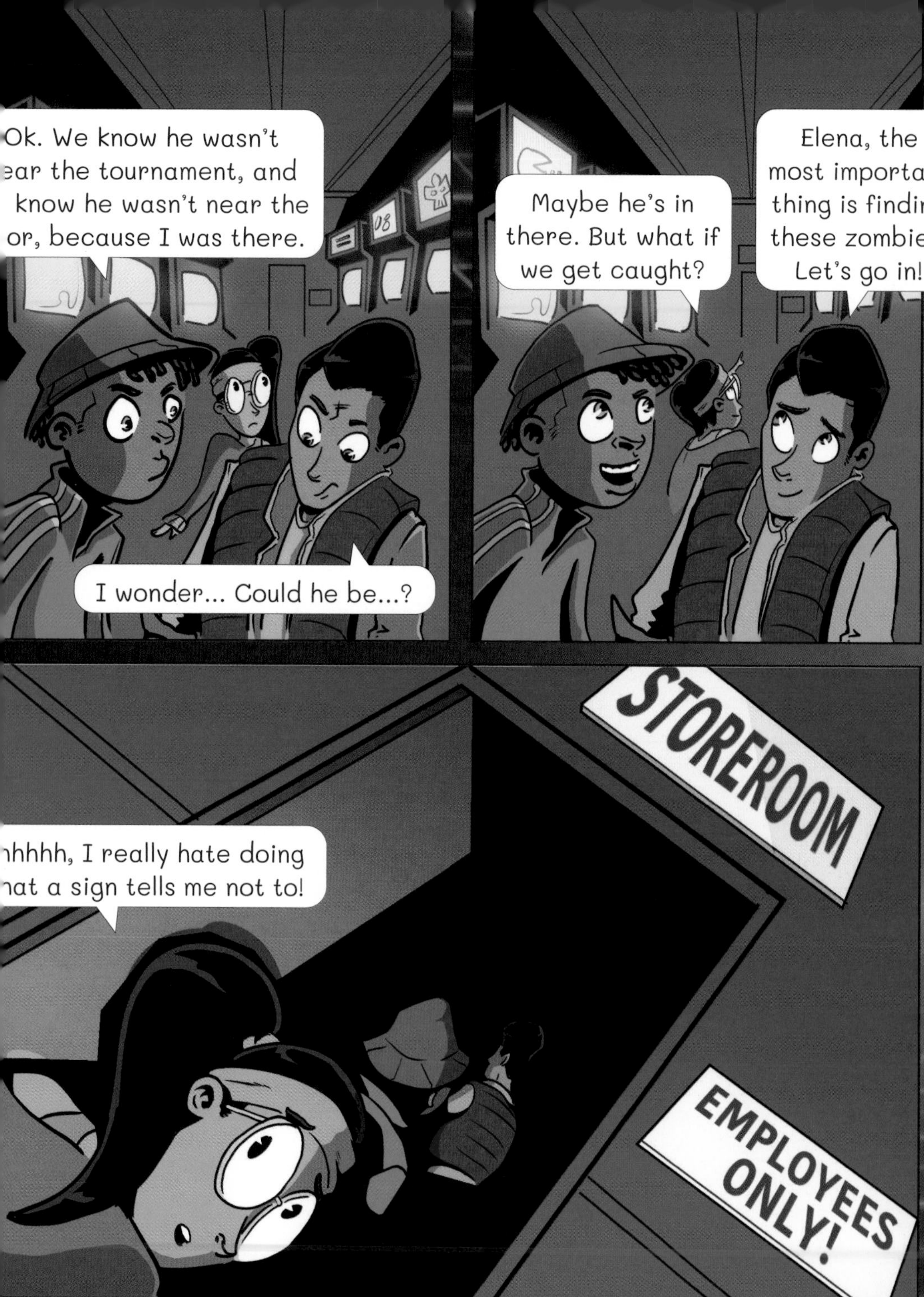
Ok. We know he wasn't ear the tournament, and know he wasn't near the or, because I was there.
I wonder... Could he be...?
Maybe he's in there. But what if we get caught?
Elena, the most important thing is finding these zombies! Let's go in!
STOREROOM
hhhh, I really hate doing at a sign tells me not to!
EMPLOYEES ONLY!

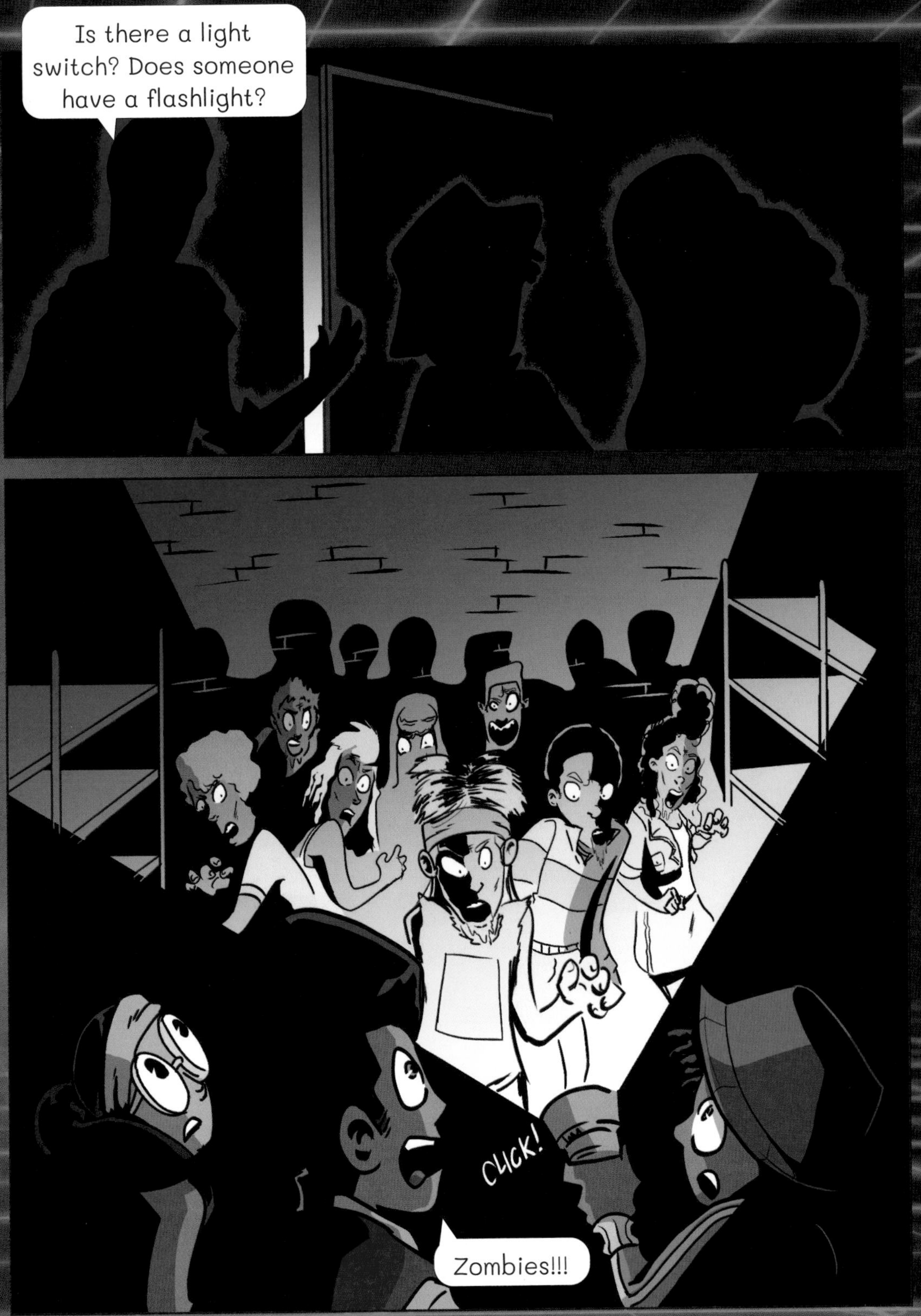
Is there a light switch? Does someone have a flashlight?
CLICK!
Zombies!!!

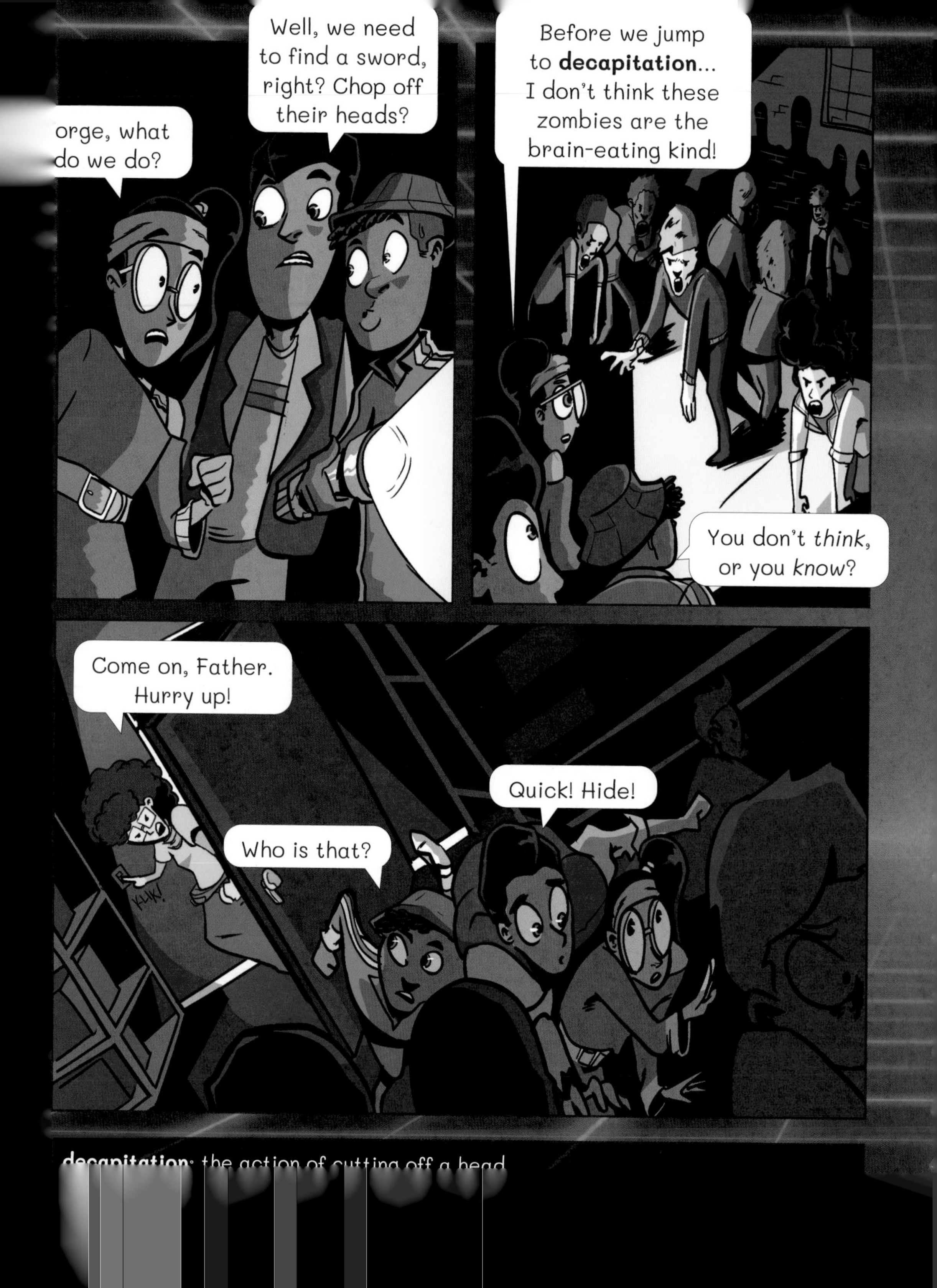
orge, what do we do?
Well, we need to find a sword, right? Chop off their heads?
Before we jump to **decapitation**... I don't think these zombies are the brain-eating kind!
You don't *think*, or you *know*?
Come on, Father. Hurry up!
Quick! Hide!
Who is that?

decapitation: the action of cutting off a head

WHAT ARE ZOMBIES?

Zombies are the undead. This means they are dead but they act alive. They are humans who have been **reanimated**. But how did they get that way?

* Sometimes zombies spread their condition through bites.

* Sometimes a spell creates a zombie.

* They follow noise and scent to find people.

How can you spot a zombie?

* Zombies eat people.

* Zombies have **decomposing** skin.

* They walk slowly, limp, and are clumsy.

* You'll hear terrible moaning and groaning noises.

* They never get tired or need to stop.

* They sometimes move in packs.

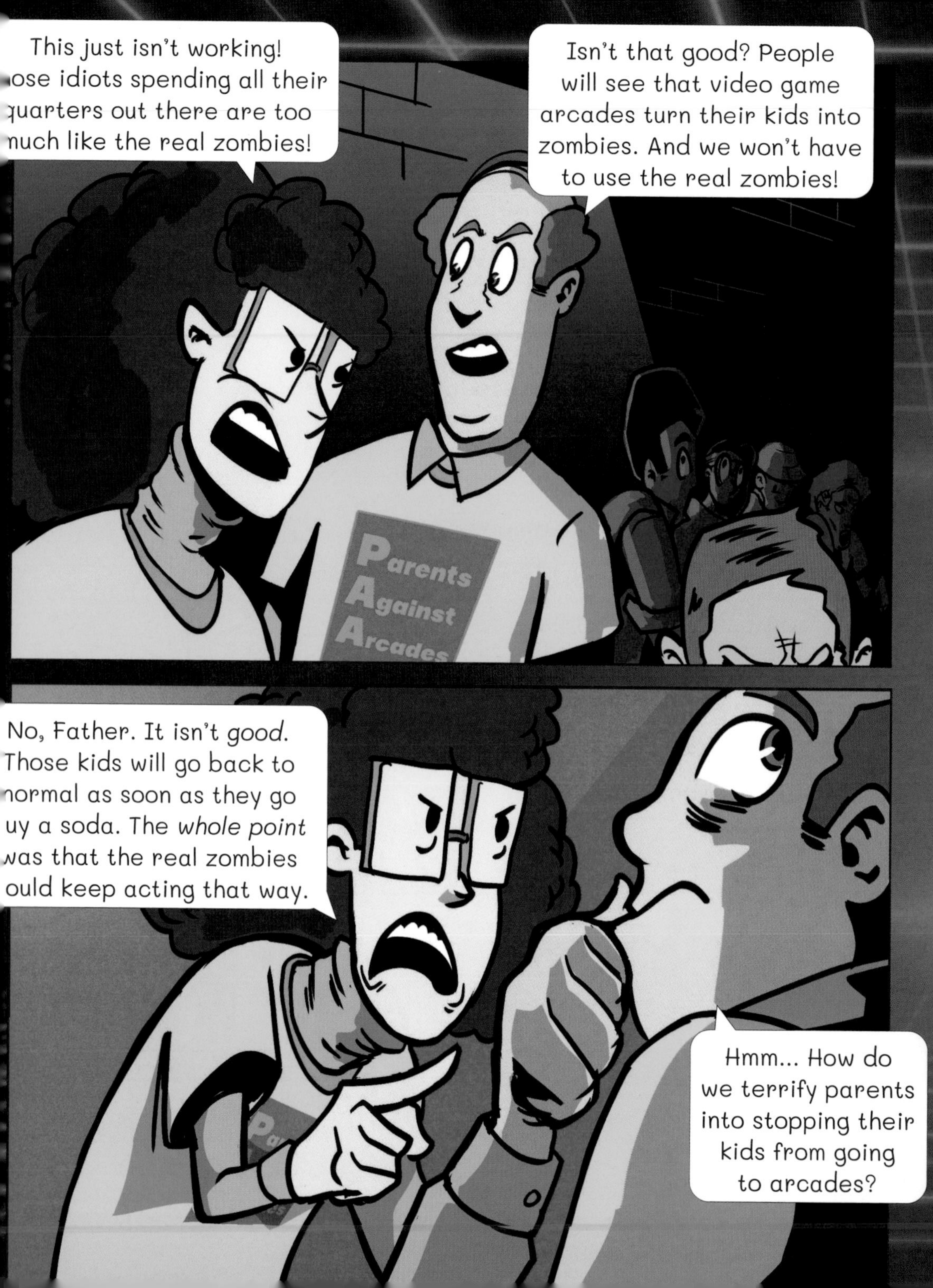
This just isn't working! ose idiots spending all their quarters out there are too uch like the real zombies!
Isn't that good? People will see that video game arcades turn their kids into zombies. And we won't have to use the real zombies!
Parents Against Arcades
No, Father. It isn't *good*. Those kids will go back to ormal as soon as they go uy a soda. The *whole point* as that the real zombies ould keep acting that way.
Hmm... How do we terrify parents into stopping their kids from going to arcades?

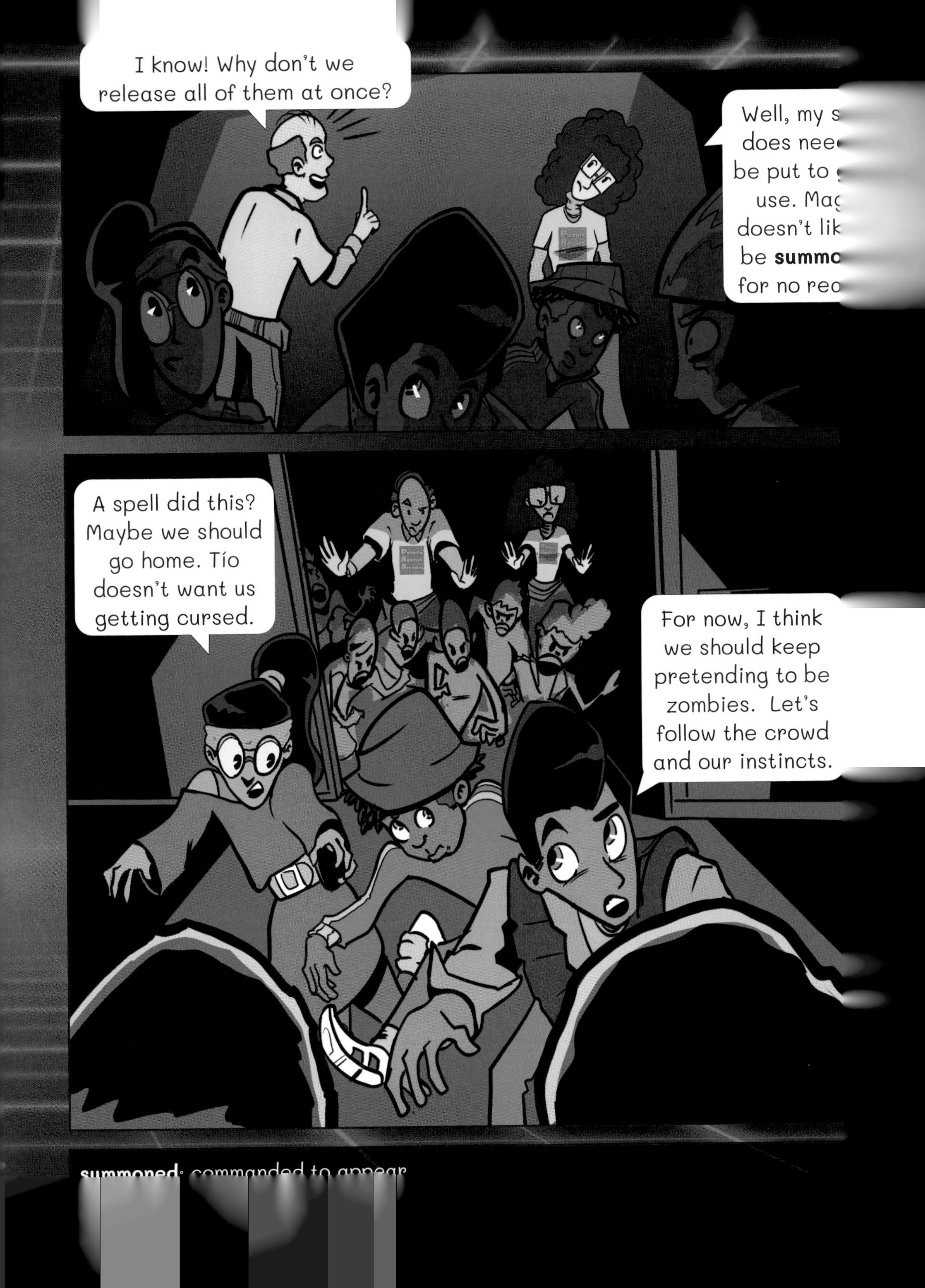
I know! Why don't we release all of them at once?
Well, my s does nee be put to use. Ma doesn't lik be summo for no rea
A spell did this? Maybe we should go home. Tío doesn't want us getting cursed.
For now, I think we should keep pretending to be zombies. Let's follow the crowd and our instincts.

summoned: commanded to appear

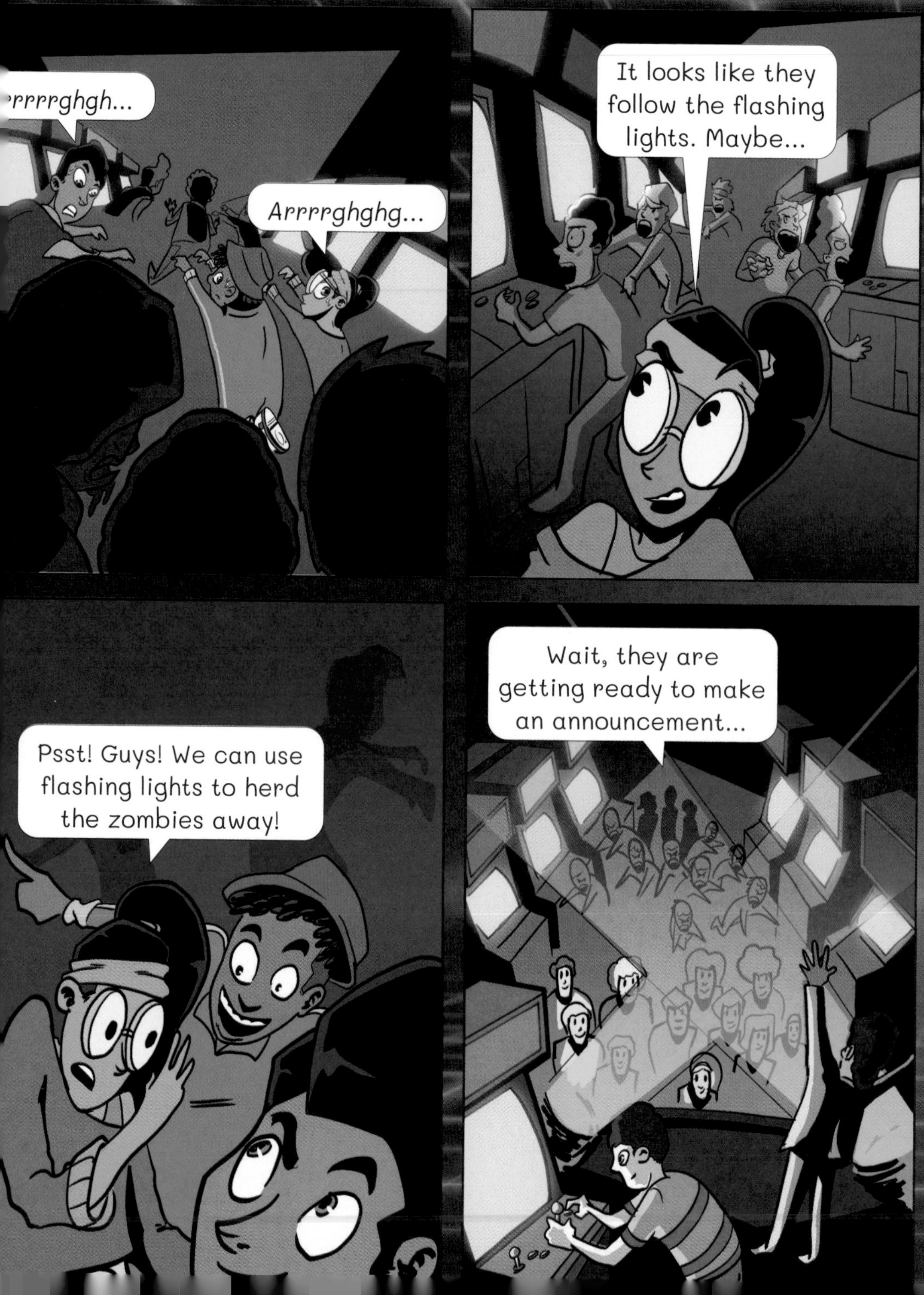
rrrrghgh...
Arrrrghghg...
It looks like they follow the flashing lights. Maybe...
Psst! Guys! We can use flashing lights to herd the zombies away!
Wait, they are getting ready to make an announcement...

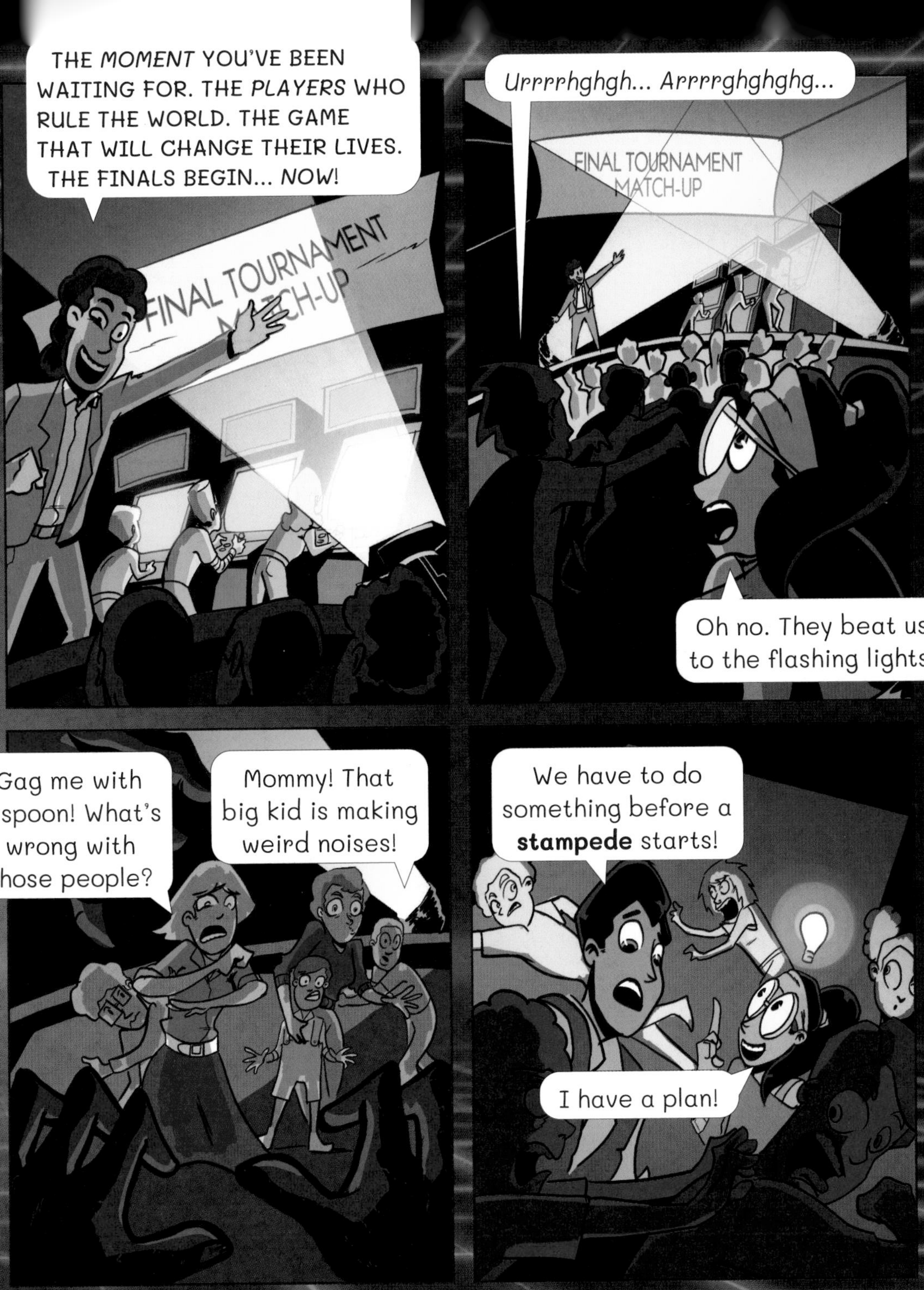
THE *MOMENT* YOU'VE BEEN WAITING FOR. THE *PLAYERS* WHO RULE THE WORLD. THE GAME THAT WILL CHANGE THEIR LIVES. THE FINALS BEGIN... *NOW*!
FINAL TOURNAMENT MATCH-UP
Urrrrhghgh... Arrrrghghghg...
FINAL TOURNAMENT MATCH-UP
Oh no. They beat us to the flashing lights!
Gag me with a spoon! What's wrong with those people?
Mommy! That big kid is making weird noises!
We have to do something before a **stampede** starts!
I have a plan!

stampede: a sudden rush or movement of many people or animals

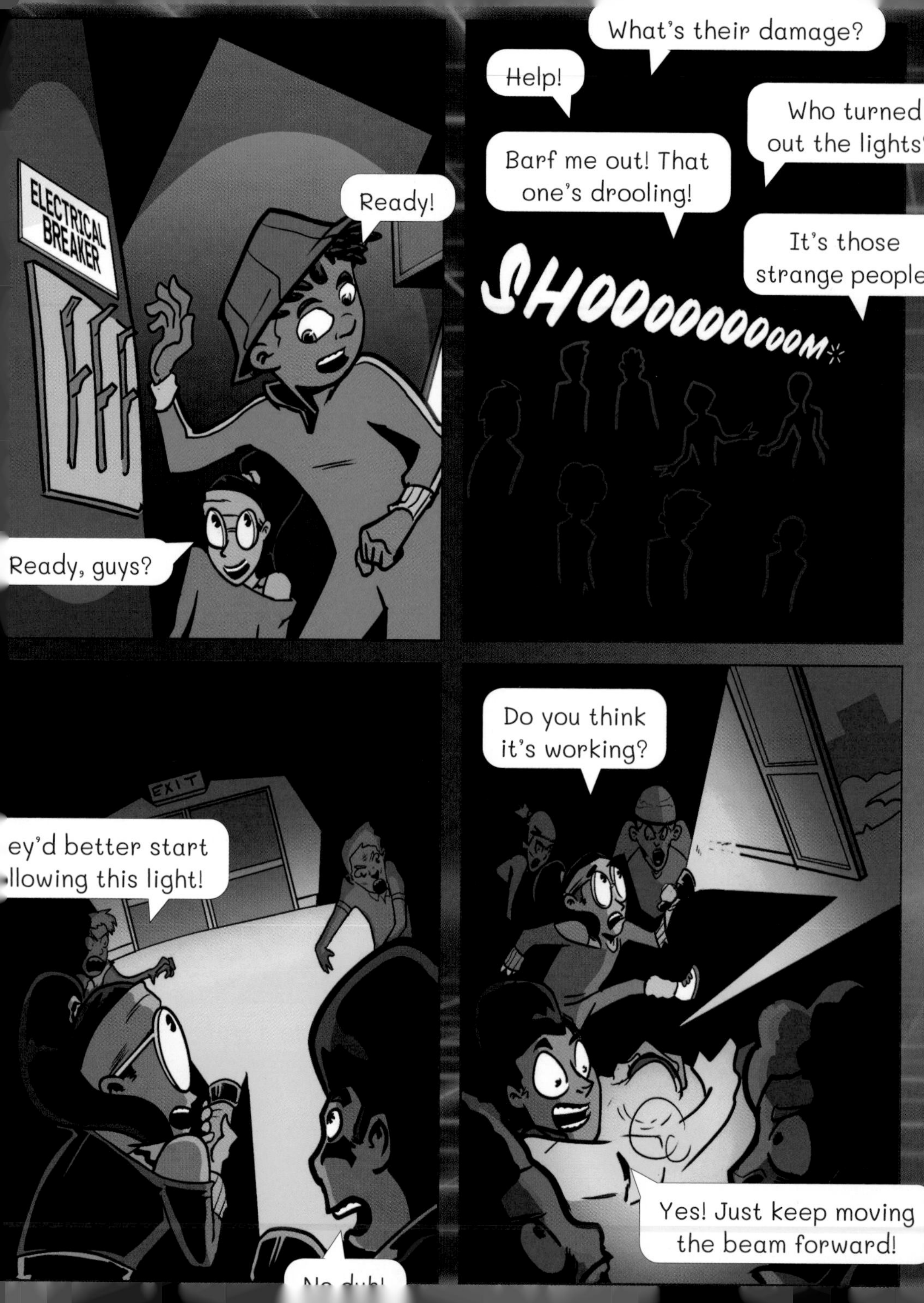
Ready, guys?
Ready!
ELECTRICAL BREAKER
What's their damage?
Help!
Who turned out the lights?!
Barf me out! That one's drooling!
It's those strange people!
SHOOOOOOOOOOM
EXIT
ey'd better start llowing this light!
Do you think it's working?
Yes! Just keep moving the beam forward!

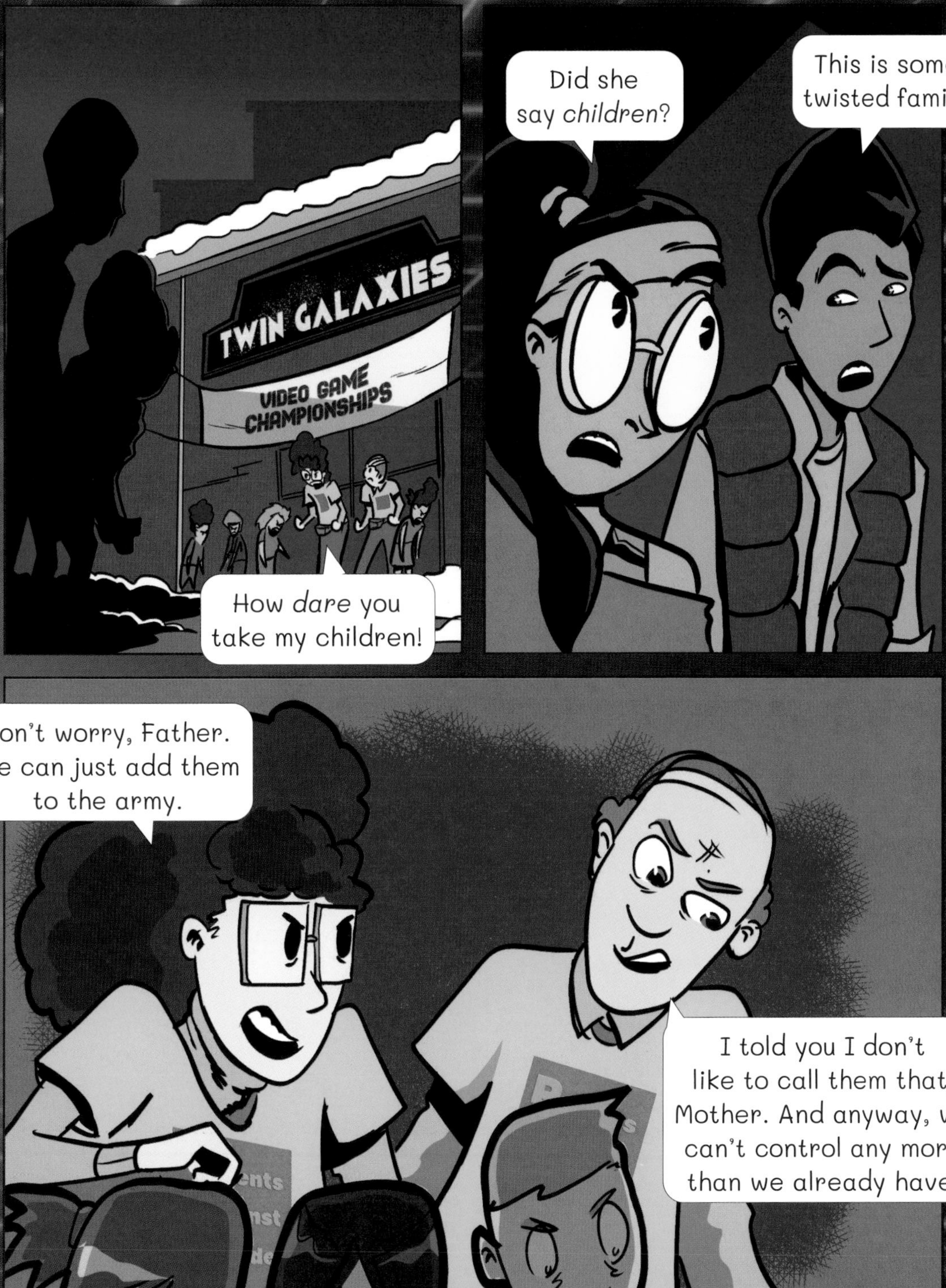
TWIN GALAXIES
VIDEO GAME CHAMPIONSHIPS
How *dare* you take my children!
Did she say *children*?
This is some twisted family.
Don't worry, Father. We can just add them to the army.
I told you I don't like to call them that, Mother. And anyway, we can't control any more than we already have.

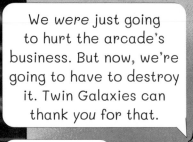

We *were* just going to hurt the arcade's business. But now, we're going to have to destroy it. Twin Galaxies can thank *you* for that.
While we're at it, we're going to destroy you for **meddling**!
Go after them! And EAT BRAINS!
Parents Against Arcades
WIN GALAXIES
Oh no! I guess this kind of zombie *can* be dangerous!
Braaaaaaiiiiiinnnnns...
RUN!
Can't let Elena have *all* the bright ideas.

meddling: interfering

SPLATTO!
Parents Against Arcades
YOINK!
Got it!
Go back... to the storage room!
No! First we have to break the spell, or these kids will be trapped!
YOINK!
For such a nervous kid, you sure save the day a lot!

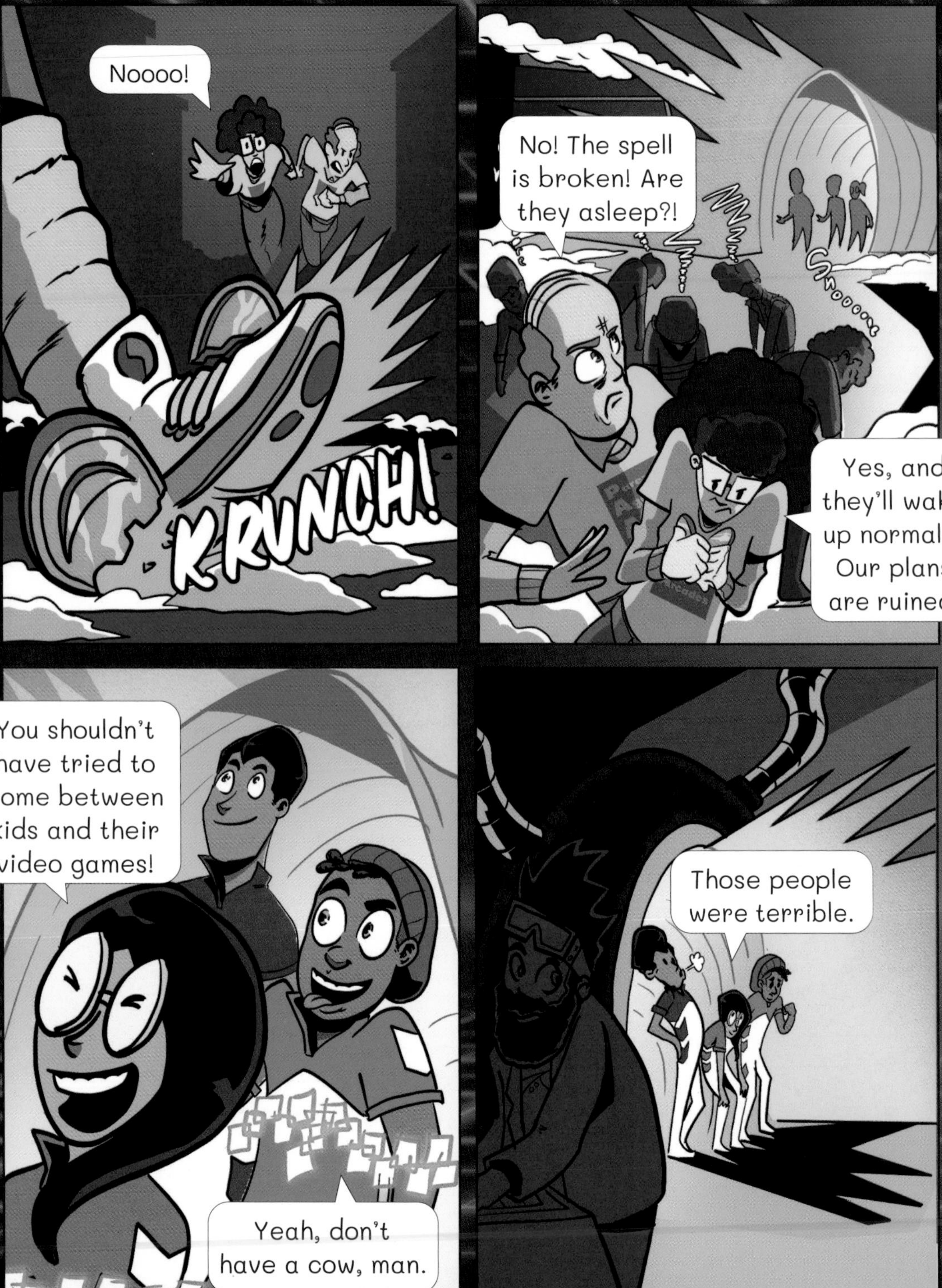
Noooo!
KRUNCH!
No! The spell is broken! Are they asleep?!
Yes, and they'll wake up normal... Our plans are ruined!
You shouldn't have tried to come between kids and their video games!
Yeah, don't have a cow, man.
Those people were terrible.

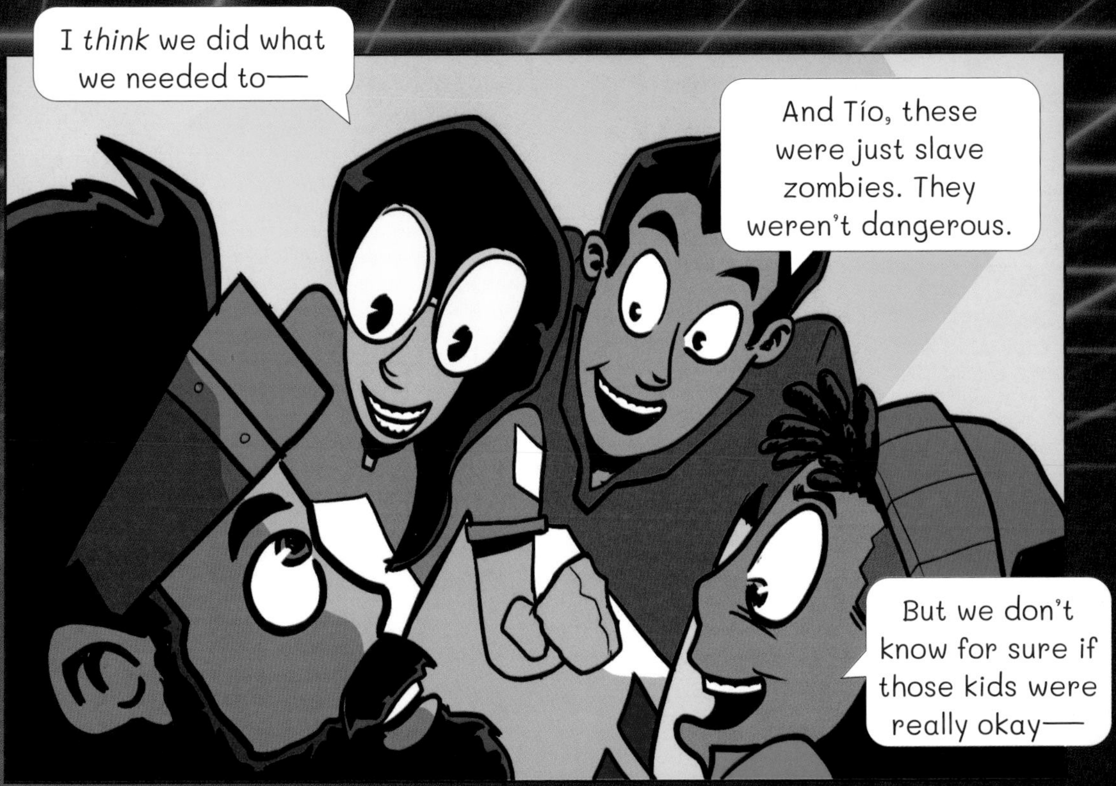
I *think* we did what we needed to—
And Tío, these were just slave zombies. They weren't dangerous.
But we don't know for sure if those kids were really okay—

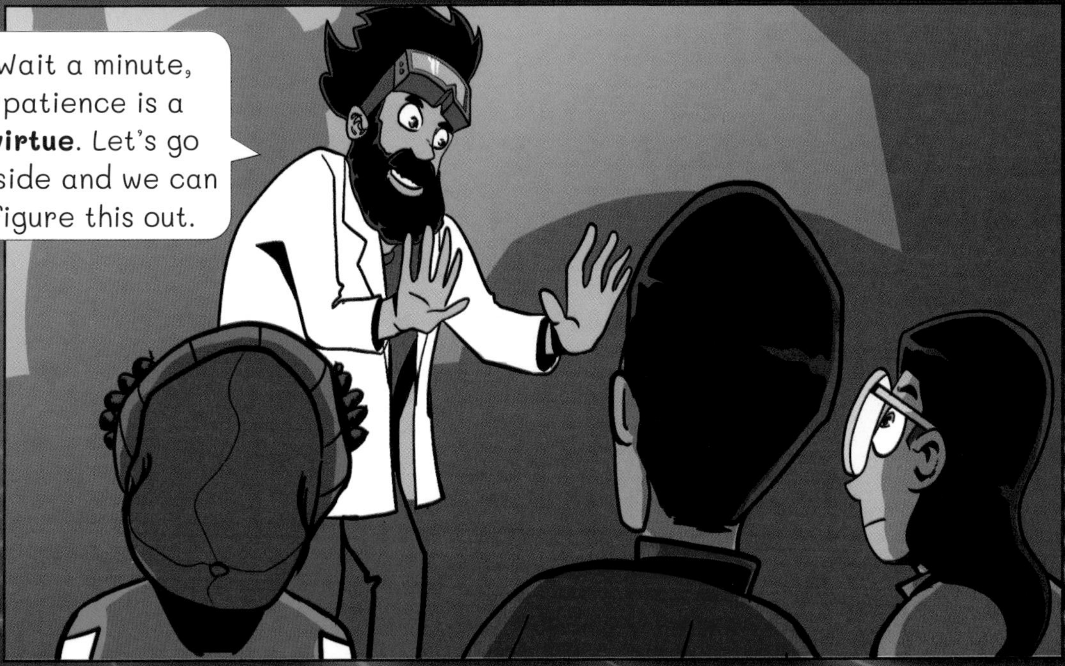
Wait a minute, patience is a **virtue**. Let's go inside and we can figure this out.

virtue: a good quality

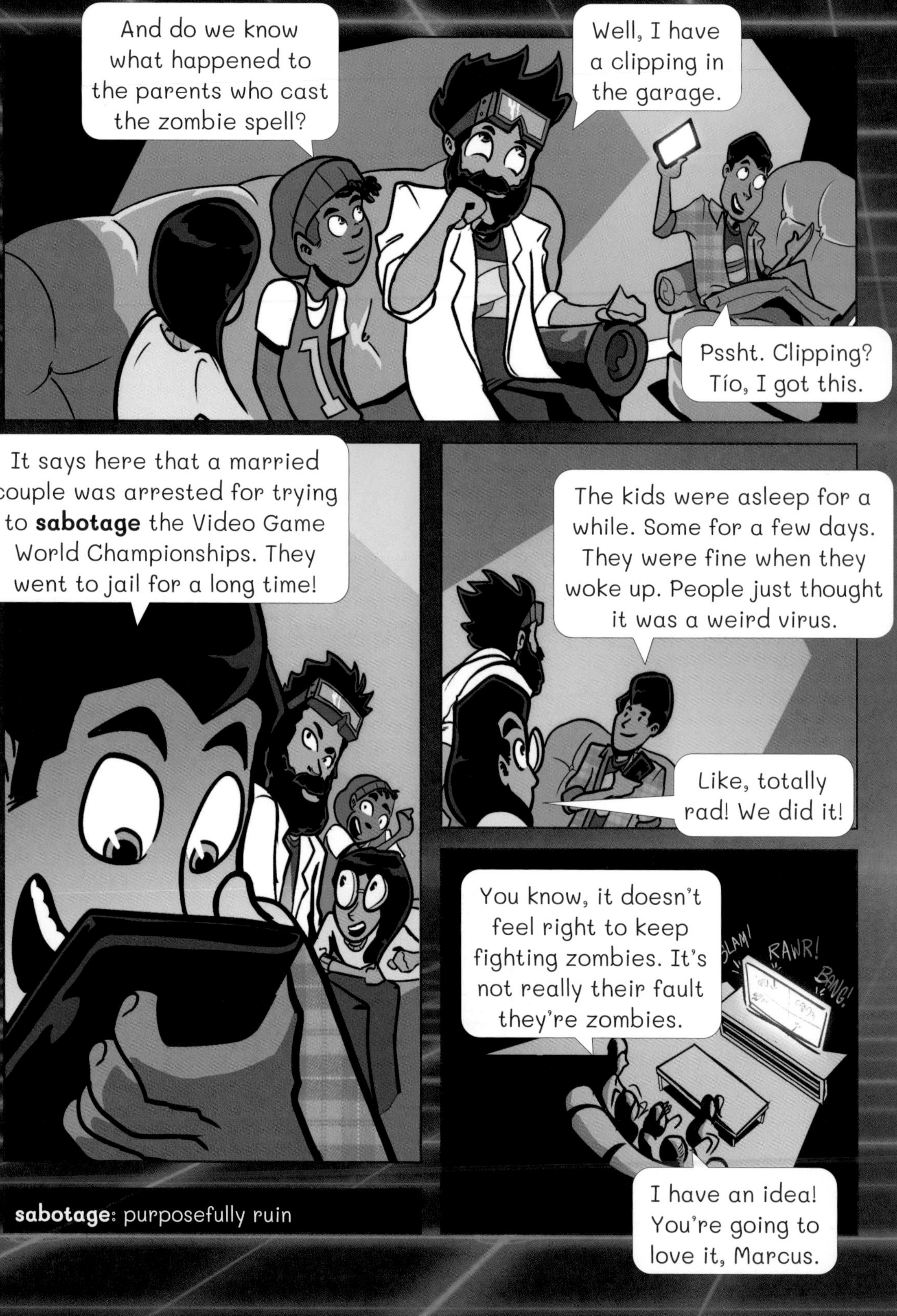
And do we know what happened to the parents who cast the zombie spell?
Well, I have a clipping in the garage.
Pssht. Clipping? Tío, I got this.
It says here that a married couple was arrested for trying to **sabotage** the Video Game World Championships. They went to jail for a long time!
The kids were asleep for a while. Some for a few days. They were fine when they woke up. People just thought it was a weird virus.
Like, totally rad! We did it!
You know, it doesn't feel right to keep fighting zombies. It's not really their fault they're zombies.
SLAM!
RAWR!
BANG!
I have an idea! You're going to love it, Marcus.

sabotage: purposefully ruin

SURVIVAL TIPS

To escape a zombie, you have to run. The best way to survive is to prepare.

* Get fit.

* Build running skills.

* Do weight training.

* Learn **martial arts**.

* If you're on the run, don't hide in a car.

* Avoid getting trapped in small spaces where zombies can surround you.

* Wherever you hide, make sure there is enough food and water to last 14 to 90 days.

* If you can't run, and you have to fight, stand against a wall. Or stand back-to-back with someone.

* Make sure no zombies can get behind you. Don't use weapons that take time to use. This gives zombies time to bite you.

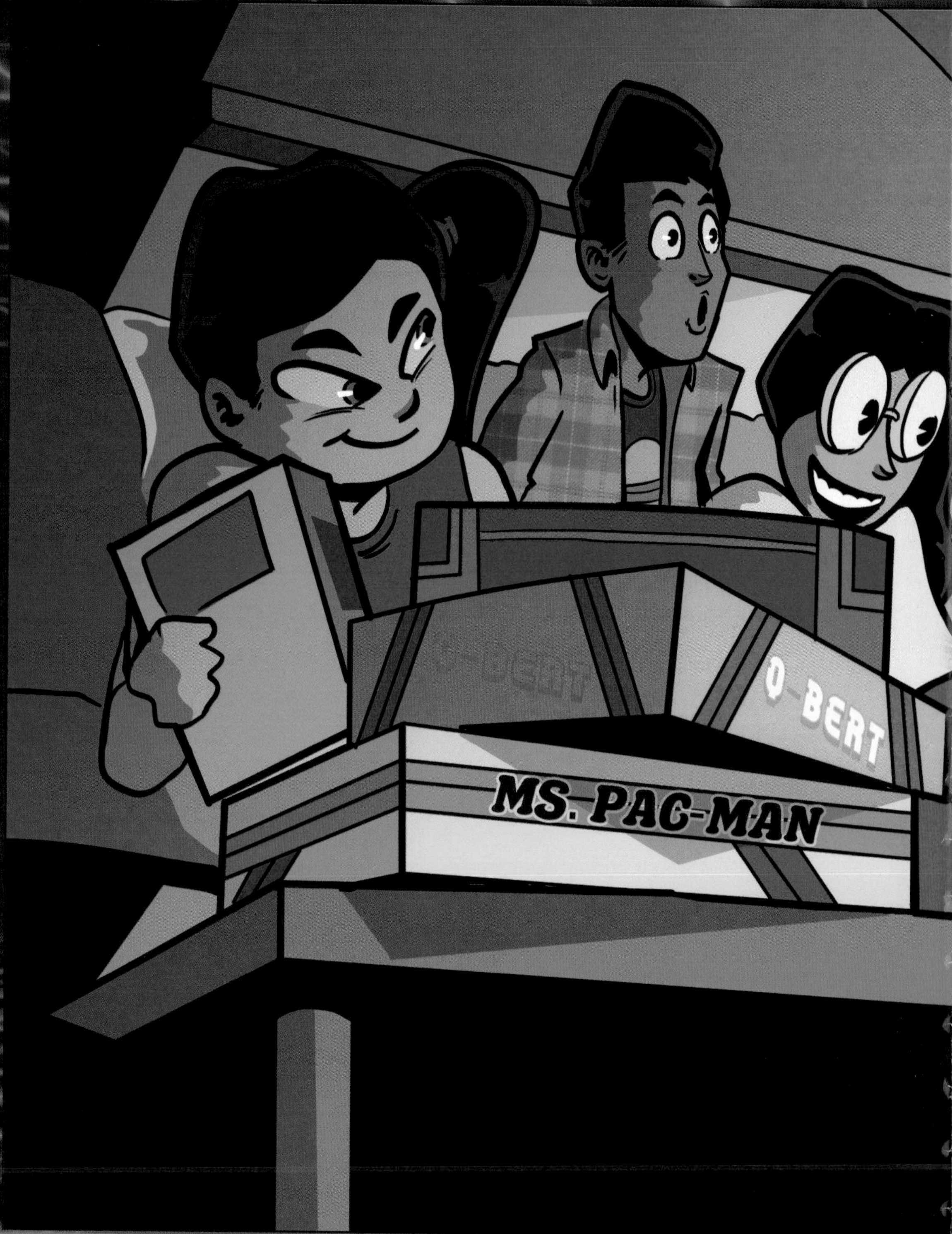
Q-BERT
Q-BERT
MS. PAC-MAN

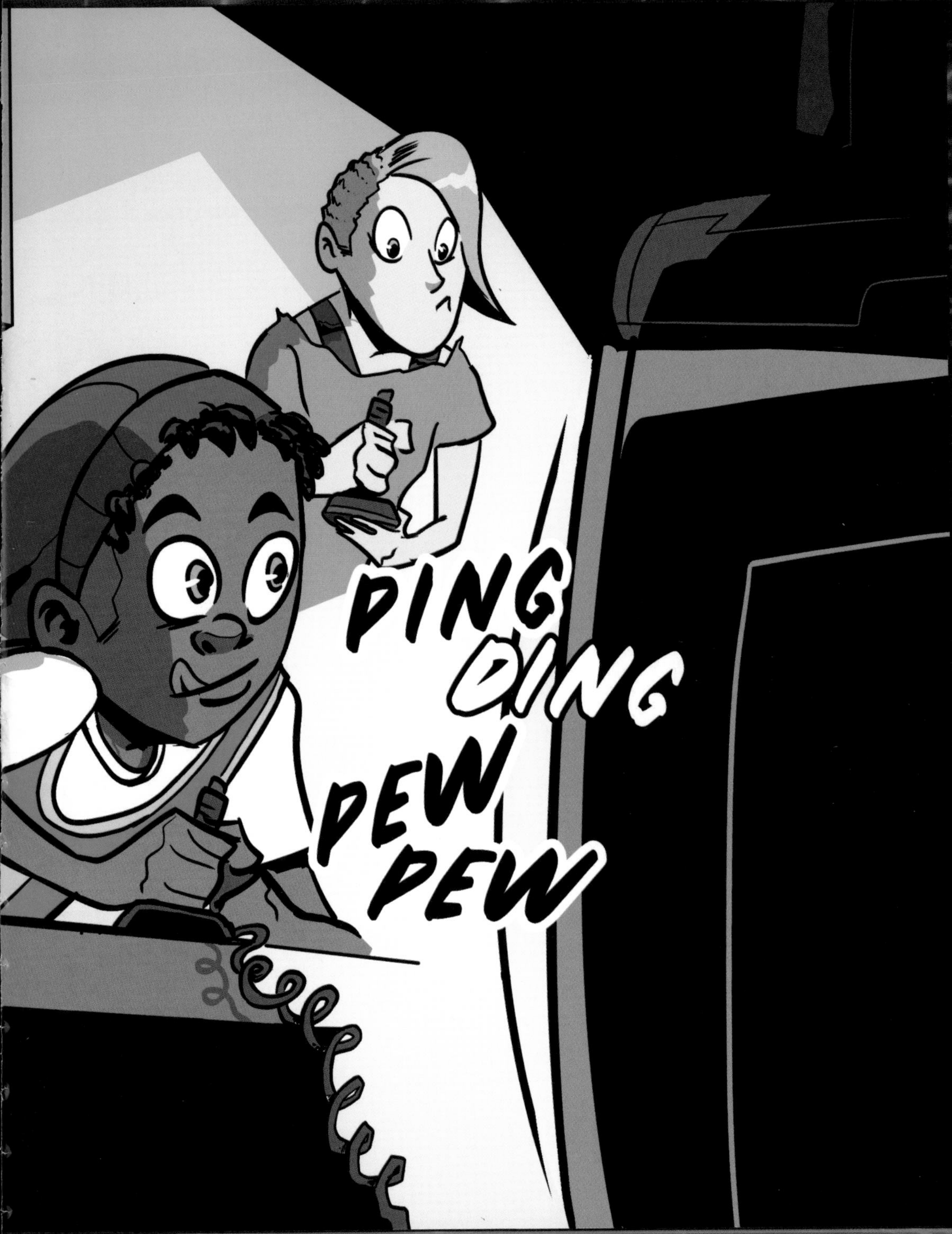
DING DING
PEW PEW

CREATE YOUR OWN GAME

You don't need to have special coding skills to create your own game that everyone can play. You can make your own board game with a few simple materials.

You'll need:

* A large sheet of paper, which will be the playing board

* Construction paper for making individual player characters and possible playing cards

* Different colored pens

* Scissors

* Dice

Now you need to make some decisions.

* What is the theme or story of your game? Are players going to make their way through a haunted forest? Or rescue a King and Queen from invading forces?

* Draw a path for players to follow. You can create a maze of squares, or maybe players hop from circle to circle.

* Remember to create obstacles for players to overcome.

* Use your scissors to create cards that give players funny or frustrating instructions. It's all up to you!

When you're done creating your game, invite friends and family to play with you.

LEARN MORE

BOOKS

Hansen, Dustin. *Game On!: Video Game History from Pong and Pac-Man to Mario, Minecraft, and More.* New York, NY: Feiwel & Friends, 2016.

Otfinoski, Steven. *The Cold War.* New York, NY: Scholastic, 2018.

WEBSITES

Ducksters, "The Cold War for Kids"
https://www.ducksters.com/history/cold_war/summary.php

Museum of Play, "Video Game History Timeline"
https://www.museumofplay.org/about/icheg/video-game-history/timeline

Smithsonian, "Video Game History"
https://www.si.edu/spotlight/the-father-of-the-video-game-the-ralph-baer-prototypes-and-electronic-games/video-game-history

THE MONSTER HUNTER TEAM

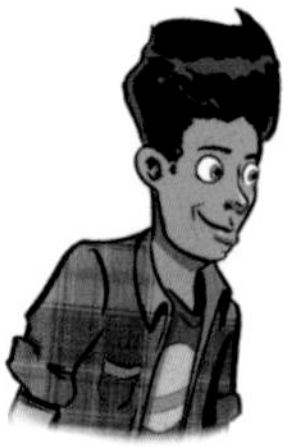

JORGE

TÍO HECTOR'S NEPHEW, JORGE, LOVES MUSIC. AT 16 HE IS ONE OF THE OLDEST MONSTER HUNTERS AND LEADER OF THE GROUP.

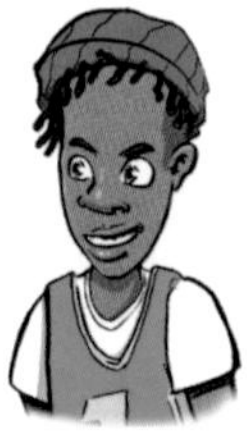

MARCUS

MARCUS IS 14 AND IS WISE BEYOND HIS YEARS. HE IS A PROBLEM SOLVER, OFTEN GETTING THE GROUP OUT OF STICKY SITUATIONS.

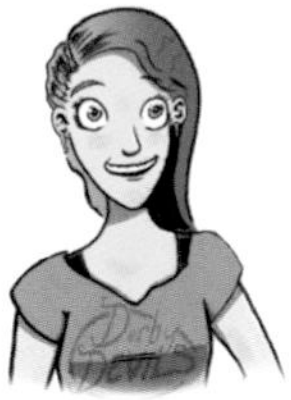

FIONA

FIONA IS FIERCE AND PROTECTIVE. AT 16 SHE IS A ROLLER DERBY CHAMPION AND IS ONE OF JORGE'S CLOSEST FRIENDS.

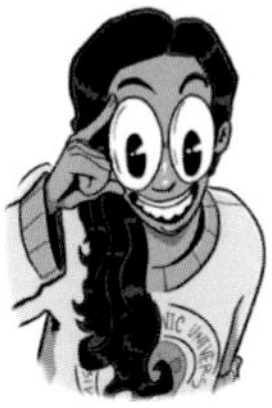

ELENA

ELENA IS JORGE'S LITTLE SISTER AND TÍO HECTOR'S NIECE. AT 14, SHE IS THE HEART AND SOUL OF THE GROUP. ELENA IS KIND, THOUGHTFUL, AND SINCERE.

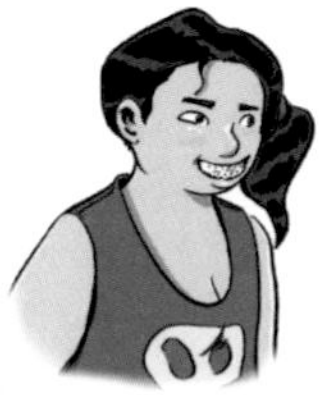

AMY

AMY IS 15. SHE LOVES BOOKS AND HISTORY. AMY AND ELENA SPEND ALMOST EVERY WEEKEND TOGETHER. THEY ARE ATTACHED AT THE HIP.

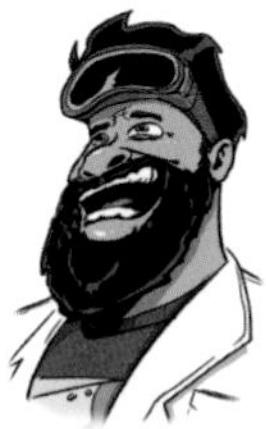

TÍO HECTOR

JORGE AND ELENA'S TÍO IS THE MASTERMIND BEHIND THE MONSTER HUNTERS. HIS TIME TRAVEL MACHINE MAKES IT ALL POSSIBLE.

GLOSSARY

commercial (kuh-MER-shul) meant to be bought and sold

decapitation (dee-kap-ih-TAY-shu) the action of cutting off a head

decomposing (dee-kum-POH-zing) the process of decaying

income inequality (IN-kum in-ee-KWAH-lih-tee) the gap between the richest and the poorest people

martial arts (MAR-shul ARTS) sports, often from East Asia, that began as self-defense skills

reanimated (ree-AN-ih-may-ted) brought back to life

sabotage (SA-buh-tahj) purposefully ruin

stampede (stam-PEED) a sudden rush or movement of many people or animals

summoned (SUH-mund) commanded to appear

tío (TEE-oh) Spanish for "uncle"

VCRs (VEE-SEE-ARZ) videocassette recorders used for recording shows off of a television or for watching shows and movies

virtue (VER-choo) a good quality

wits (WITS) mental sharpness

INDEX